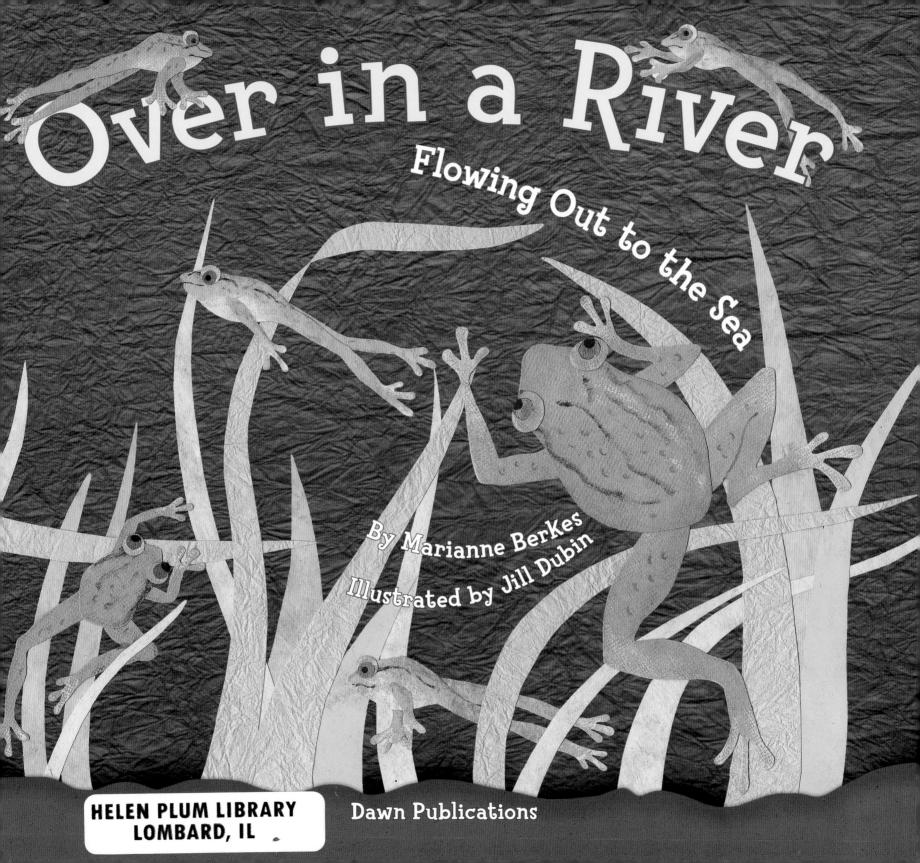

Over in a River

Flowing Out to the Sea

By Marianne Berkes

Illustrated by Jill Dubin

Dawn Publications

Over in a river
Where the warm waters run
Lived a mother manatee
And her little *calf* one.

"Paddle" said the mother.
"I paddle," said the one.
So they paddled in a river
Where the warm waters run.

St. Johns River

Over in a river
Where the cattails grew
Lived a mother blue heron
And her little *chicks* two.

"Stand," said the mother.
"We stand," said the two.
So they stood like statues
Where the cattails grew.

Hudson River

2

Over in a river
Flowing out to the sea
Lived a mother wild salmon
And her little *smolts* **three**.

"Splash," said the mother.
"We splash," said the **three**.
So they splashed down a river
Flowing out to the sea.

Columbia River

3

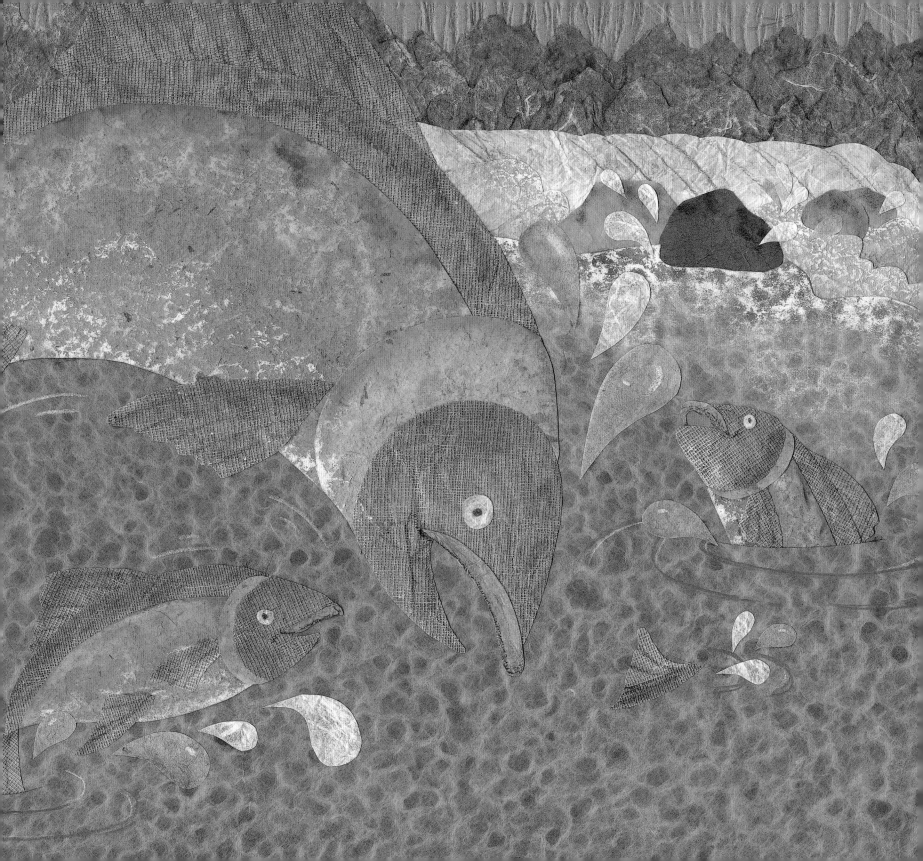

Over in a river
In a nest on the shore
Lived a mother mallard duck
And her little *ducklings* four.

"Waddle," said the mother.
"We waddle," said the four.
So they waddled to a river
From their nest on the shore.

St. Lawrence River

4

Over in a river
Where they swallowed prey alive
Lived a mother water snake
And her little *hatchlings* five.

"Slither," said the mother.
"We slither," said the five.
So they slithered by a river
Where they swallowed prey alive.

Ohio River

5

Over in a river
In their lodge built with sticks
Lived a busy mother beaver
And her little *kits* six.

"Gnaw," said the mother.
"We gnaw," said the six.
So they gnawed on bark
Near their lodge built with sticks.

Colorado River

Over in a river
Darting up toward heaven,
Lived a mother dragonfly
And her *dragonflies* seven.

"Whirl," said the mother.
"We whirl," said the seven.
So they whirled above a river
Darting up toward heaven.

Rio Grande River

7

Over in a river
Where they could communicate
Lived a furry mother muskrat
And her little *kits* eight.

"Squeal," said the mother.
"We squeal," said the eight.
So they squealed in a river
Where they could communicate.

Missouri River

8

Over in a River
In the warm sunshine
Lived a mother tree frog
And her little *froglets* nine.

"Hop," said the mother.
"We hop," said the nine.
So they hopped to a river
In the warm sunshine.

Sacramento River

Over in a river
Where they played in their den
Lived a father river otter
And his little pups ten.

"Slide," said the father.
"We slide," said the ten.
So they slid in the mud
And they played in their den.

Mississippi River

10

Columbia River

Missouri River

Mississippi River

Sacramento River

Colorado River

Rio Grande River

Over in a river
Flowing out to the sea
River animals have homes,
Swimming wild and flying free.

Find the river babies
From ten to one,
Then go back and start over
Cause this rhyme isn't done.

Over in a river
You can spy with your eyes
To find ten hidden creatures—
Every page has a surprise!

Fact or Fiction?

The animals in this story behave as they have been portrayed — muskrats *squeal*, manatees *paddle*, and dragonflies *whirl*. That's a fact! But do they have the number of babies as in this rhyme? No, that is fiction! Do the babies live in the rivers shown on the map? Yes, they live approximately where shown, but they often live in lots of other rivers too.

Baby animals are cared for in very different ways, depending upon the species. Beaver and otter babies are cared for by both the mother and the father and they live with their family until they reach maturity, usually between one and two years of age. Only a mother manatee cares for her calf and it often rides on her back until it gets too big. A mother mallard also cares for her ducklings after they are born, while a mother dragonfly lays eggs in water and leaves. Nature has very different ways of ensuring the survival of species.

Rivers Matter!

Water that falls as rain or snow can either flow across the top of the ground or soak into the ground. Often it flows underground, perhaps coming to the surface again as a spring. Water from a spring or small creek joins a larger stream, which joins another, until many smaller streams make up a river.

Rivers are always part of a river system—a *watershed*—with many *tributaries*. A watershed includes all the land area that drains to a particular point in a river. The main rivers and the tributaries are given different names. For example, the Missouri River and the Ohio River are tributaries of the Mississippi River. But they are all part of the same watershed. Occasionally, rivers like the Truckee River flowing from California into Nevada go into a desert and simply evaporate—disappear! But almost always, a river empties into the ocean at a place called the *mouth* of the river. There it often slows down and spreads out onto a *delta*, which is usually a good place for animals to live.

As you've just read in the story, rivers are home to many different kinds of fish and wildlife. Rivers and other wet places provide food and shelter, and are especially important during times of breeding and migration. Rivers are very important to humans too. They provide water for drinking, irrigation, transportation, recreation, and electrical power. Rivers are vital to the health and wellbeing of humans.

About the Rivers and Hidden Animals

The United States has over 250,000 rivers. Canada has even more than the U.S. Here are the rivers featured in this book.

The ST. JOHNS RIVER is the longest river in Florida. When winter comes, manatees paddle into warmer waters of this river from the Atlantic coastline. Did you find the hidden *alligator*?

The **HUDSON RIVER** rises in the Adirondack Mountains of New York and flows south between New York and New Jersey to the Atlantic Ocean. Great blue herons stalk for prey while a *snapping turtle* hides.

The **COLUMBIA RIVER** rises in the Rocky Mountains of British Columbia, Canada. It flows between Washington and Oregon, gathering water from tributaries from Idaho and Montana before reaching the Pacific Ocean. Wild salmon that swim there should watch out for the hidden *bear*!

The **ST. LAWRENCE RIVER** is one of the longest rivers in North America. It drains water from the entire Great Lakes area as far away as Minnesota, and forms part of the boundary between New York and Ontario, Canada. Mallards nest throughout this region. Do you see the *largemouth bass*?

The **OHIO RIVER** forms in Pennsylvania and gathers water primarily from Ohio, Indiana, West Virginia, Kentucky, and Tennessee—so much water that the Ohio River is the largest tributary of the Mississippi by volume. The illustrated Northern water snake is a common kind of water snake that lives here. Did you see the *Canada goose*?

The **COLORADO RIVER** is the principal river of the southwestern United States, gathering water from Colorado, Utah, Nevada, Arizona, and New Mexico, and flowing through Mexico into the Gulf of California. Beavers live along this 1,450 mile long river. Did you notice the *belted kingfisher*?

The **RIO GRANDE** rises in southwestern Colorado, flows through New Mexico and forms the border between Texas and Mexico before emptying into the Gulf of Mexico. Lots of dragonflies hover overhead while *trout* swim below.

The **MISSOURI RIVER** drains water from a huge area of the Great Plains and Rocky Mountains, and flows east and south for 2,341 miles before entering the Mississippi River. Muskrats live on the banks of the river. Did you see a *snail* in the mud?

The **SACRAMENTO RIVER** is the longest river in California, flowing from the slopes of Mount Shasta to San Francisco Bay, which opens to the Pacific Ocean. Pacific tree frogs live in wet areas all around the river while the *pond skater* runs across its surface.

The **MISSISSIPPI RIVER** is the main river of the largest water river system in North America. It starts in Minnesota and either borders or cuts through ten states, covering 2,530 miles before reaching the Gulf of Mexico. Combined with all its tributaries, the Mississippi River system drains water from 31 states and two Canadian provinces. Otters along its banks eat *crayfish*. Did you see one?

About the Animals in the Story

MANATEES are marine mammals that migrate to different areas as water temperatures change. If they remain in water that is too cold, they will die. So when temperatures drop below 65 degrees in the ocean, manatees *paddle* to warmer rivers and estuaries. They move very slowly, chewing on sea grasses or other freshwater vegetation. All the chewing they do wears out their teeth, so new teeth grow at the back of their jaws and move forward as the worn-down teeth in front fall out.

GREAT BLUE HERONS are large wading birds with long legs and long necks that fold into an S-curve when flying. Herons can reach speeds of 30 miles per hour. They often live around rivers and bays in colonies called rookeries. A slow methodical stalker, herons will often *stand* motionless in shallow water hunting fish, frogs, crayfish, and snakes. They spear their prey with their long pointed bill and usually swallow it whole. They sometimes also eat small mammals.

SALMON live in the ocean until it is time to *spawn* (lay eggs) in freshwater rivers and streams. Babies grow inside the eggs, and are on their own after they hatch. The newly hatched fish are called *fry*. As they grow they are called *smolts* and live from one to three years before migrating to the salty ocean, They travel far out into the ocean where they live for another one to five years, depending on species, feeding on krill, shrimp and other small fish. They then return to the very same river and stream where they were born, *splashing* upstream against great odds—sometimes as far as 2,000 miles—to propagate the next generation of salmon.

MALLARDS are wild ducks that "dabble"—that is, they float on the surface of the water, tipping tail-up and head-down to find food underwater. The male (drake) has a brilliant glossy green head and bright yellow bill. The female (hen) is a mottled brown. The hen builds a nest on land and lays an average of nine eggs. After the ducklings hatch, they *waddle* to a river or other water where they learn to dabble for vegetation and small crustaceans.

WATER SNAKES, unlike many other snakes, do not lay eggs. Instead, the female carries the eggs inside her body and gives birth to live young—as many as thirty babies at one time. But as soon as they are born, the hatchings are on their own. Northern water snakes are one of the most abundant snakes throughout most of the eastern half of the U.S. and Ontario, Canada. They are not poisonous, but are often confused with the cottonmouth, which is. They *slither* to the water to eat fish and amphibians, and swallow their prey whole. They are good swimmers.

BEAVERS are furry rodents with large, flat tails and long, sharp teeth. Their teeth are so strong that they can chew through large tree trunks. They love to eat bark, along with leaves, roots, twigs and water plants. Their front teeth continually grow, so a beaver must *gnaw* on trees and branches to keep them sharp, and from growing too big. Beavers are famous for building dams to make ponds out of mud, stones, and sticks. In the pond they build dome-shaped homes called *lodges*. The entrance is always underwater. Both parents care for one to four kits born in the spring. Kits usually stay with the parents for two years.

DRAGONFLIES, sometimes known as "hawks of the insect world," catch many flying insects in mid-air, often over water. They have two very large eyes and four (two pairs) of long, transparent wings. Each wing is controlled independently of the others, giving dragonflies the ability to fly backward, straight up or down, stop, hover, and *whirl* in mid-air. Dragonflies lay their eggs in calm water. The larva (nymph) swims and lives there from one to three years. Then it climbs out of the water onto a plant stem, takes its first-ever breath, sheds its hard outer shell, and grows wings! This amazing process is called *metamorphosis*. Once out of water, these "baby" dragonflies—already fully grown—live only a few weeks.

MUSKRATS often live in burrows dug into the bank alongside a waterway that has abundant cattails and other tall plants. The entrance is underwater. Sometimes they locate their homes in marshy areas, in which case they build lodges made of mud and sticks up to three feet high, and plug the entrance with vegetation. They like to eat cattails and water lilies. Muskrats have poor hearing and vision and communicate with squeaks and *squeals*. Sometimes they give off a very strong smell, called *musk*, which is how they got their name. Their thick fur is nearly waterproof and keeps them warm. They are very good swimmers, but can't move quickly on land, and will retreat to their burrow if threatened.

PACIFIC TREE FROGS are small frogs whose call sounds like "ribbit." They usually do not climb as high as most tree frogs and move about by *hopping*. Like all amphibians, tree frogs spend their lives near the water where they lay thousands of eggs attached to vegetation. The eggs hatch into tadpoles, which swim in the water until they change into frogs and are able to live on land.

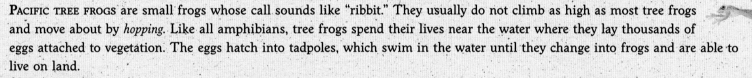

RIVER OTTERS are sleek, furry mammals with webbed paws that live in rivers, streams, and ponds. Newborn pups are cared for by both mother and father. Their dens have openings above the water in summer, but in winter they can only be entered underwater. River otters are expert swimmers and can stay underwater for up to four minutes. They are active all year long and are kept warm by their dense fur and high metabolism. Otters are very playful. They chase each other and *slide* down mud paths. They eat fish, crustaceans, amphibians, insects, birds, and small mammals.

Tips from the Author

This book offers wonderful opportunities for extended activities. Here are some suggestions:

SING AND ACT: While you sing, act out what each animal does: *paddle, splash, waddle, whirl,* and so on. Hear the "Over in the Meadow" melody at: http://www.dawnpub.com/our-authorsillustrators/marianne-berkes/ Scroll down under "media" to "Audio .mp3 files."

CUT-OUTS AND STICK PUPPETS: Using print-outs from http://www.enchantedlearning.com/biomes/pond/pondlife.shtml, color and cut out each animal and glue onto tongue depressors for stick puppets. Or place on a flannel board as you read or sing the story. Older students can place them on a flannel board map of North America in the appropriate river. Note that some rivers flow in Canada and Mexico.

COUNT THE CATTAILS: Cattails are plants that are usually found in streams and along rivers where there is shallow, slow-moving, or standing water. Young children can count them on each page.

SAME AND DIFFERENT: Compare a main animal in the book with the hidden animal on the same page using a Venn diagram. http://www.graphic.org/venbas.html

ANIMAL CLASSIFICATION: How many animals in the book are mammals? How many reptiles? Insects? Fish?

DISCUSS:

- What were the ten main animals called as babies? Which one does not have a "baby" name? Can you guess baby names for the hidden animals?
- Think of an action verb for each hidden animal to show how it might behave, e.g. an alligator *snaps*!
- Older students can write a description of a hidden animal similar to what the author has done for the main animals in the story.
- Did the author have to know about the hidden animals before asking the illustrator to put them on specific pages? For example, why did the author pair the bear with the salmon but not with the manatee?

Food is a basic need for all living things. Which river animals are *herbivores*? Which ones are *carnivores*? Are there any *omnivores*?

Discover more in books and on the internet

Water Dance by Thomas Locker (Sandpiper, 2002)
Where the River Begins by Thomas Locker (Puffin, 1993)
A River Ran Wild by Lynne Cherry (Sandpiper, 2002)
Water, Water Everywhere by Cynthia Ovebeck (Sierra Club, 1995)

American Rivers is an organization that works to protect rivers and educate us about them. Their web site has lots of interesting educational material. http://www.americanrivers.org/rivers/about/

Creek Freaks and **Save Our Streams** are both hands-on watershed education and action program of the Izaak Walton League. Learn how to monitor streams, post photos and data, and download the free Creek Freaks curriculum at http://www.iwla.org/

KidsGeo.com has kid-friendly information about rivers and streams. http://www.kidsgeo.com/geography-for-kids/0151-rivers-and-streams.php

Enchanted Learning offers wonderful resources, including activities about river animals and a labeled map of rivers. http://www.enchantedlearning.com/usa/outlinemaps/riverslabeled/

Which rivers empty into the Gulf of Mexico?

I take care of the babies with my mate and am playful. Who am I?

For the answers go to www.dawnpub.com, click on "Teachers/ Librarians" and "Downloadable Activities." Scroll down to the cover of this book. You will also find more of Marianne's curriculum-connection activities, including reproducible river animal bookmarks.

Tips from the Illustrator

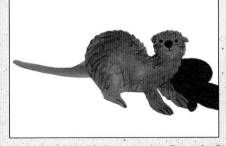

As soon as I get the text of the book from the author, pictures start forming in my mind—cattails swaying in the breeze, colorful dragonflies, and otters with mud splashing all around them.

Before I even start to draw an animal, I research images of them. To draw the river otter I look at as many as 50 photographs, then sketch a very rough pencil drawing of each otter and its placement in the illustration as it slides in the mud. Next I redraw each otter, making sure to get all the details correct. The face, the hands and feet, the tail, and the body shape all have to look like river otters. I put each separate otter into the whole picture. I draw on tracing paper so when I put it all together I can overlap some and move them around until the entire picture looks good.

I also draw the hidden animal and find a good spot for it within the illustration. I'm usually very careful where I put each piece down so I don't lose any as I work. I wasn't so careful with the crayfish. When I was ready to glue it into place, it was nowhere to be found! I hunted on my desk, the floor, and even checked my sleeves. I was on the verge of cutting a new one when, happily, it emerged from the chaos of paper around me.

I use cut paper collages for my illustrations. After I complete the sketch I choose which paper I'm going to use. Most of the paper comes from art supply stores. I'm always looking for new and interesting paper. I compare the paper I plan to use for the animals with the paper for the background. Since the otters are brown and the mud they're sliding in is brown, it was a challenge to make sure the animals stood out enough. The color and texture of the papers help distinguish the otters from the mud. I enhanced the fur of the otters and the edges of the mud with pastels. Pastels are soft chalk that comes in many different colors.

I then make copies of each piece of the illustration. Using the copy as a pattern, I carefully cut from the paper I select. Then I glue the components together. I use a small amount of glue or it can get messy very quickly. First I make the animals, then I lay them on the papers I select for the background. I can see how the animals look on different papers so I can make changes before I glue everything down.

It's exciting to take the words and create a picture and see how it all comes together as a finished book. Take a look at the "tips" I wrote in the other books in this series — *Over in the Arctic*, *Over in Australia*, and *Over in the Forest* and you'll have lots of ideas of cut-paper projects to do and how to do them.

Over in a River

Sung to the tune "Over in the Meadow"

Traditional Tune
Words by Marianne Berkes

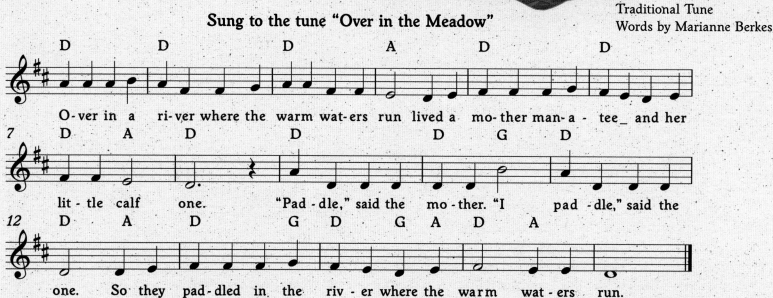

O- ver in a ri- ver where the warm wat- ers run lived a mo- ther man- a- tee_ and her

lit- tle calf one. "Pad- dle," said the mo- ther. "I pad- dle," said the

one. So they pad- dled in the riv- er where the warm wat- ers run.

2. Over in a river
Where the cattails grew
Lived a mother blue heron
And her little chicks two.

"Stand," said the mother.
"We stand," said the two.
So they stood like statues
Where the cattails grew.

3. Over in a river
Flowing out to the sea
Lived a mother wild salmon
And her little smolts three.

"Splash," said the mother.
"We splash," said the three.
So they splashed down a river
Flowing out to the sea.

4. Over in a river
In a nest on the shore
Lived a mother mallard duck
And her little ducklings four.

"Waddle," said the mother.
"We waddle," said the four.
So they waddled to a river
From their nest on the shore.

5. Over in a river
Where they swallowed prey alive
Lived a mother water snake
And her little hatchlings five.

"Slither," said the mother.
"We slither," said the five.
So they slithered by a river
Where they swallowed prey alive.

6. Over in a river
In their lodge built with sticks
Lived a busy mother beaver
And her little kits six.

"Gnaw," said the mother.
"We gnaw," said the six.
So they gnawed on bark
Near their lodge built with sticks.

7. Over in a river
Darting up toward heaven,
Lived a mother dragonfly
And her dragonflies seven.

"Whirl," said the mother.
"We whirl," said the seven.
So they whirled above a river
Darting up toward heaven.

8. Over in a river
Where they could communicate
Lived a furry mother muskrat
And her little kits eight.

"Squeal," said the mother.
"We squeal," said the eight.
So they squealed in a river
Where they could communicate.

9. Over in a River
In the warm sunshine
Lived a mother tree frog
And her little froglets nine

"Hop," said the mother.
"We hop," said the nine.
So they hopped to a river
In the warm sunshine.

10. Over in a river
Where they played in their den
Lived a father river otter
And his little pups ten.

"Slide," said the father.
"We slide," said the ten.
So they slid in the mud
And they played in their den.

MARIANNE BERKES has spent much of her life as a teacher, children's theater director and children's librarian. She knows how much children enjoy "interactive" stories and is the author of many entertaining and educational picture books that make a child's learning relevant. Reading, music and theater have been a constant in Marianne's life. Her books are also inspired by her love of nature. She hopes to open kids' eyes to the magic found in our natural world. Marianne now writes full time. She also visits schools and presents at conferences. She is an energetic presenter who believes that "hands on" learning is fun. Her website is www.MarianneBerkes.com.

JILL DUBIN uses cut paper to create her whimsical illustrations. She develops each illustration by combining color, pattern and texture. Detail and depth are added with pastel and colored pencil. She has illustrated over 30 children's books. Jill received her BFA from Pratt Institute in Brooklyn, NY. She lives in Atlanta, GA. www.JillDubin.com

DEDICATIONS

In loving memory of my parents, Anne and Harry Staffhorst, and boating adventures in City Island, NY, where my friends and I spent many happy times in an amazing little boat named "Nellybelle" that my Dad built for us. — MB

To the two new little guys in our family, Atticus and Teddy. With lots of love. — JD

Book design and computer production by Patty Arnold, *Menagerie Design & Publishing*

DAWN PUBLICATIONS

12402 Bitney Springs Road
Nevada City, CA 95959
530-274-7775
nature@dawnpub.com

Special thanks to Media Specialist Nancy Hecht and students at Clay Springs Elementary for the photo on the "Tips from the Author" page, and to Ken Rosenberg, with the Conservation Science Program at Cornell Lab of Ornithology, for his assistance with selection of birds.

Library of Congress Cataloging-in-Publication Data

Berkes, Marianne Collins.
 Over in a river : flowing out to the sea / by Marianne Berkes ; illustrated by Jill Dubin.
      pages cm
 Summary: "This counting book in the style of 'Over in the Meadow' presents various riparian habitat animals and their offspring in ten North American rivers, from a mother manatee 'and her little calf one' in the St. Johns River to a father river otter 'and his little pups ten' in the Mississippi. Endnotes present facts, activities, and related games"-- Provided by publisher.
 ISBN 978-1-58469-329-1 (hardback) -- ISBN 978-1-58469-330-7 (pbk.) [1. Stories in rhyme. 2. Stream animals--Fiction. 3. Animals--Infancy--Fiction. 4. Counting.] I. Dubin, Jill, illustrator. II. Title.
 PZ8.3.B4557Os 2013
 [E]--dc23   2013009250

Manufactured by Regent Publishing Services, Hong Kong
Printed July, 2013, in ShenZhen, Guangdong, China

10 9 8 7 6 5 4 3 2 1
First Edition

ALSO BY MARIANNE BERKES

Over in the Ocean: In a Coral Reef — With outstanding style, this book portrays a vivid community of marine creatures. **Also available as an App!**

Over in the Jungle: A Rainforest Rhyme — As with *Ocean*, this book captures a rain forest teeming with animals. **Also available as an App!**

Over in the Arctic: Where the Cold Winds Blow — Another charming counting rhyme introduces creatures of the tundra.

Over in Australia: Amazing Animals Down Under — Australian animals are often unique, many with pouches for the babies. Such fun!

Over in the Forest: Come and Take a Peek — Follow the tracks of forest animals, but watch out for the skunk!

Seashells by the Seashore — Kids discover, identify, and count twelve beautiful shells to give Grandma for her birthday.

Going Around the Sun: Some Planetary Fun — Earth is part of a fascinating "family" of planets. Here's a glimpse of the "neighborhood."

Going Home: The Mystery of Animal Migration — Many animals migrate "home," often over great distances. This winning combination of verse, factual language, and beautiful illustrations is a solid introduction.

What's in the Garden?—Healthy fruits and vegetables grow in a garden bursting with life and are much more interesting when children know where they come from. And a few tasty recipes can start a lifetime of good eating.

SOME OTHER NATURE AWARENESS BOOKS FROM DAWN PUBLICATIONS

The E-I-E-I-O Books follow the adventures of young Jo, granddaughter of Old MacDonald, as she discovers the delights of the pond, woods, and garden on Old MacDonald's farm. *Jo MacDonald Saw a Pond*, *Jo MacDonald Hiked in the Woods*, and *Jo MacDonald Had a Garden*. E—I—E—I—O!

Molly's Organic Farm is based on the true story of homeless cat that found herself in the wondrous world of an organic farm. Seen through Molly's eyes, the reader discovers the interplay of nature that grows wholesome food.

The "BLUES" Series — A comical team of cartoon bluebirds are crazy about REAL birds, and become quite the birdwatchers in *The BLUES Go Birding Across America*, *The BLUES Go Birding at Wild America's Shores*, and *The BLUES Go Extreme Birding*.

The "Mini-Habitat" Series — Beginning with the insects to be found under a rock (*Under One Rock: Bugs, Slugs and Other Ughs*) and moving on to other small habitats (around old logs, on flowers, cattails, cactuses, and in a tidepool), author Anthony Fredericks has a flair for introducing children to interesting "neighborhoods" of creatures. Field trips between covers!

Dawn Publications is dedicated to inspiring in children a deeper understanding and appreciation for all life on Earth. You can browse through our titles, download resources for teachers, and order at www.dawnpub.com, or call 800-545-7475.